A NOTE TO PARENTS

When your children are ready to "step into reading," giving them the right books is as crucial as giving them the right food to eat. **Step into Reading Books** present exciting stories and information reinforced with lively, colorful illustrations that make learning to read fun, satisfying, and worthwhile. They are priced so that acquiring an entire library of them is affordable. And they are beginning readers with a difference—they're written on five levels.

Early Step into Reading Books are designed for brand-new readers, with large type and only one or two lines of very simple text per page. **Step 1 Books** feature the same easy-to-read type as the Early Step into Reading Books, but with more words per page. **Step 2 Books** are both longer and slightly more difficult, while **Step 3 Books** introduce readers to paragraphs and fully developed plot lines. **Step 4 Books** offer exciting nonfiction for the increasingly independent reader.

The grade levels assigned to the five steps—preschool through kindergarten for the Early Books, preschool through grade 1 for Step 1, grades 1 through 3 for Step 2, grades 2 through 3 for Step 3, and grades 2 through 4 for Step 4—are intended only as guides. Some children move through all five steps very rapidly; others climb the steps over a period of several years. Either way, these books will help your child "step into reading" in style!

For Patterson,
with love and fond memories of the
prenatal hiccups
—L.W.

For Susan, Jenny, and Kim Havlka
—J. H.

Text copyright © 1999 by Lee Wardlaw Jaffurs.
Illustrations copyright © 1999 by Joan Holub.
All rights reserved under International and Pan-American Copyright Conventions.
Published in the United States by Random House, Inc., New York, and simultaneously
in Canada by Random House of Canada Limited, Toronto.

www.randomhouse.com/kids

Library of Congress Cataloging-in-Publication Data
Wardlaw, Lee, 1955–
Hector's hiccups / by Lee Wardlaw ; illustrated by Joan Holub.
    p.   cm. — (Step into reading. A Step 2 book)
SUMMARY: When Hector gets the hiccups, his brother and sister try everything they can
think of to make them go away.
ISBN 0-679-89200-1 (pbk.) — ISBN 0-679-99200-6 (lib. bdg.)
[1. Hiccups—Fiction. 2. Brothers and sisters—Fiction.] I. Holub, Joan, ill.   II. Title.
III. Series: Step into reading. Step 2 book. PZ7.W2174He 1999 [E]—dc21 98-41046

Printed in the United States of America 10 9 8 7 6 5 4 3 2

STEP INTO READING, RANDOM HOUSE, and the Random House colophon are registered
trademarks of Random House, Inc. The Step into Reading colophon is a trademark
of Random House, Inc.

Step into Reading®

Hector's Hiccups

By Lee Wardlaw

Illustrated by Joan Holub

A Step 2 Book

Random House New York

"Hic!" said Hector.

His brother, Carlos,

stopped drawing.

"Did you hear that?" he called.

Their sister, Maria, looked out

of the tree house.

"I didn't hear anything," she said.

"Hic-hic!" said Hector.

"I think it's coming from Hector,"
said Carlos.

Maria climbed down the tree.

"Time for a visit
from Doctor Maria,"
she said.

Maria opened her doctor kit.

"Stick out your tongue
and say *ahhh,* Hector," she said.

Hector stuck out his tongue
and said, "Hic!"

"Uh-oh," said Maria.

"Hector has the hiccups!"

"Hic! Hic-hiccup!" agreed Hector.

Maria giggled.

"He sounds like popcorn,"
she said.

"Maybe he ate a grasshopper,"
Carlos teased.

"It's hopping inside his tummy.

Like this!"

Carlos jumped up and down.

"No hopper!" said Hector.

"Hic! Hic-hiccup!"

9

"Don't worry, Hector," said Carlos.

"I have a cure for hiccups."

He scooped Hector into his arms

and plopped him on the swing.

Carlos told Hector to take

a deep breath.

"Now hold it while I count to five,"

said Carlos.

"One…two…three…"

"He's breathing through his nose,"

Maria warned.

"Are you?" Carlos asked.

"No nose!" said Hector.

"We have to start over,"

Carlos said.

Hector took another breath.

Carlos counted on his fingers.

"One...two...three...four...five!"

Hector let the air out.

"Whoosh!" he said,

and tumbled off the swing.

"How do you feel?" asked Carlos.

"Hic!" said Hector. "Hic-hiccup!"

"Some cure," Maria said with a smile.

Maria took Hector's hand.

"Come with me," she said.

"Doctor Maria has a *super* cure
for hiccups."

She led him into the kitchen.

Maria took a large paper bag

from the cupboard.

She pulled it over Hector's head.

"Take deep breaths,"

Maria said.

"In and out. In and out."

Hector wiggled his nose.

The bag smelled like oranges.

"How do you feel?"

Maria asked.

"Dark," said Hector.

"Keep taking deep breaths,"

Maria said.

Carlos tugged a pen
from his pocket.
He drew a totem pole
on one side of the bag.

"That's pretty good,"

said Maria.

Carlos drew a lady robot

on the other side of the bag.

"I think she needs a hat,"
Maria said.

"No hat!" said Hector.

"Never mind," Maria said.

"You're done."

She pulled off the bag.

Hector blinked.

"Hic! Hic-hiccup!"

"Oops," said Maria.

"Some super cure!" Carlos said.

"Do you have a better idea?"

Maria asked.

Carlos smiled.

It was a sneaky smile.

He whispered in Maria's ear.

"Oooh," she said.

Carlos patted Hector's arm.

"I have a super-*duper* cure

for hiccups," he said.

"It's in my room.

I'll be right back."

Carlos winked at Maria.

Then he raced down the hall.

"How are your hiccups?"

Maria asked.

"Are they still with us?"

"Hic!" said Hector. "Hic-hiccup!"

"They'll be gone soon,"

Maria promised.

She tapped her foot.

She drank some juice.

Then she fed the cat.

"Hic!" said Hector. "Hic-hiccup!"

"Carlos has been gone
a long time,"
Maria said.
"Let's go find him."
She led the way
down the hall.

25

Maria knocked on the door.

No answer.

Hector knocked on the door, too.

Nothing happened.

"That's funny," Maria said.

"Hic-hic!" said Hector.

"Hic-hic-hiccup!"

"We need that super-duper cure
right away," said Maria.
"Hector, open the door
and peek inside."
Hector reached up
and turned the doorknob.
He poked his head
into the bedroom.

A gorilla with wild hair,

sharp fangs,

and a smushed nose

leaped out at him.

"GROWL-ER-ROWL-ER-ROWL!"

it said.

"AAAHHH!" screamed Hector.

He turned and bumped into Maria.

"AAAHHH!" he screamed again.

Hector dashed down the hall.

He tumbled through the kitchen

and knocked over the cat food.

Then he ran into the dining room
and dived under the table.

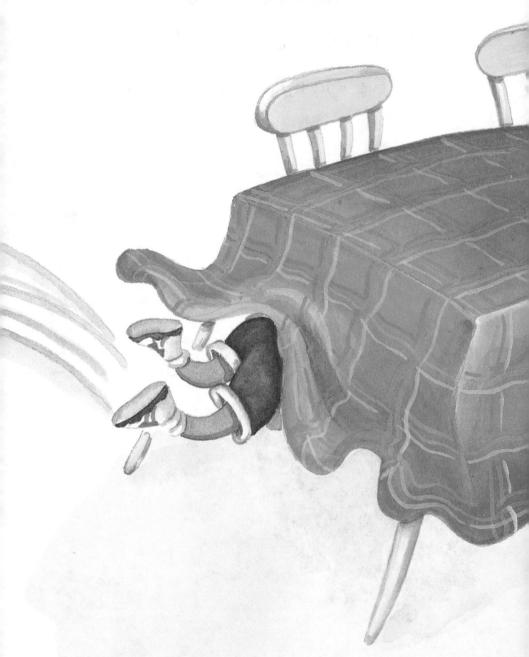

Carlos and Maria raced after him.

"I'm sorry, Hector," Carlos said.

"It's just a mask, see?"

He held up a rubber gorilla face.

"We didn't want to scare
you away,"
said Maria.
"Just your hiccups."

33

"Hic-hic-hic!" said Hector.

"HIC-HIC-HICCUP!"

"He's worse than ever," Carlos said.

"What do we do now?" asked Maria.

"Should we stand him
on his head?"
asked Carlos.
"Or," said Maria,
"maybe he should
drink a glass
of water while
hopping on one foot."

"We could scare him again,"
said Carlos.
"I have a rhino mask
in my closet."
"No rhino!" said Hector.
He started to cry.

Maria snapped her fingers.

"I've got an idea!"

She ran to Hector's room.

She looked
in his closet.

She looked in
the toy box.

Finally, she peeked
under Hector's bed.
"Aha!" she cried.

Maria pulled Señor Fur,

Hector's bear,

from his hiding place.

He wore dust bunnies

on his ears.

She brushed a cobweb

from his nose.

Maria ran back

to the dining room.

"Look who I found, Hector,"

Maria said in a soft voice.

"Let's tell Señor Fur a story."

She lifted Hector onto her lap
and gave him a hug.

"Once upon a time," Maria said,

"Señor Fur was walking in the woods.

All of a sudden, he got the hiccups.

'Hic!' he said.

'Hickety-hickety-hiccup!'"

Hector giggle-hicked.

Maria looked at Carlos for help.

"Um…Señor Fur had
a brother and a sister,"
said Carlos.
"And they tried hard
to cure his hiccups.
But nothing worked."

Then Carlos
and Maria told
Hector a story
about Señor Fur
meeting gorillas
with smushed noses.

And rhinos
wearing
paper bags.

And lady
robots that
marched around
eating oranges.

"Hey, Maria," said Carlos.

"Listen!"

"I don't hear anything,"
said Maria.

"Hector's hiccups are gone!"

said Carlos.

"We did it!" said Maria.

Carlos, Maria, and Hector

crawled out from under the table.

"How do you feel, Hector?"

Maria asked.

Hector hugged Señor Fur.

He buried his nose

in the bear's dusty head.

His nose tickled.

His nose itched.

"ACHOO!" said Hector.

"ACHOO-ACHOO-ACHOO!"

"Oh, no!" Maria cried.

Carlos laughed.

"Here we go again," he said.